Copyright © 1962, 2002 by Nord-Süd Verlag AG, Gossau Zürich, Switzerland
First published in Switzerland under the title *Der Clown sagte Nein.*
English translation copyright © 2002 by North-South Books Inc., New York

This edition published in the United States, Great Britain, Canada,
Australia, and New Zealand in 2002 by North-South Books,
an imprint of Nord-Süd Verlag AG, Gossau Zürich, Switzerland.

An earlier edition with longer text and different illustrations was
published in the United States, Great Britain, Canada,
Australia, and New Zealand in 1986 by North-South Books,
© 1986 Rada Matija AG, Staefa, Switzerland.

Distributed in the United States by North-South Books Inc., New York.

Library of Congress Cataloging-in-Publication Data is available.
A CIP catalogue record for this book is available from The British Library.
ISBN 0-7358-1552-6 (trade edition) 10 9 8 7 6 5 4 3 2 1
ISBN 0-7358-1553-4 (library edition) 10 9 8 7 6 5 4 3 2 1
Printed in Belgium

For more information about our books, and the authors and artists
who create them, visit our web site: www.northsouth.com

The Clown Said No

by
Mischa Damjan

illustrated by
Christa Unzner

translated by
Anthea Bell

North–South Books
NEW YORK/LONDON

There was a breathless hush in the circus tent when the ringmaster shouted, "Ladies and gentlemen and children of all ages! Now for our star act! Presenting the clown Petronius, and Theodore, the stubborn donkey!"

The audience clapped and cheered. The circus band began to play—but nothing happened!

The clown didn't move, and neither did the donkey.

The band played and played, and then at last they stopped.

"Jump to it, Petronius! Get a move on!" cried the ringmaster, cracking his whip impatiently. But still neither the clown nor the donkey moved.

"Jump to it, Petronius!" shouted the ringmaster, even louder than before.

There was silence. And then . . . the clown said, "No!"

Theodore the donkey flicked his ears from left to right. He was saying no, too. The audience laughed and clapped. They thought it was a very funny act.

The ringmaster didn't think it was funny at all, and he cracked his whip again.

"I'm tired of laughing and crying and playing the fool," said
Petronius calmly.

"What do you want to do then?" asked the ringmaster.

"I want to tell stories to children and poets," said Petronius.
The ringmaster swung around and yelled at the donkey,
"What about you? Are you planning to tell stories, too?"

"No, I'm going to listen to Petronius," replied the donkey
patiently. And with these words, the clown and the donkey
turned and left the ring.

This all must be part of the show, the audience told themselves, clapping.

The ringmaster announced the next act, "Here comes Ferdinand the dancing pony!"

A pony walked into the ring. The ringmaster raised his whip—but the pony said, "I'm not performing anymore. I'm not proud of being just a trained dancing pony."

The pony left the ring, too.

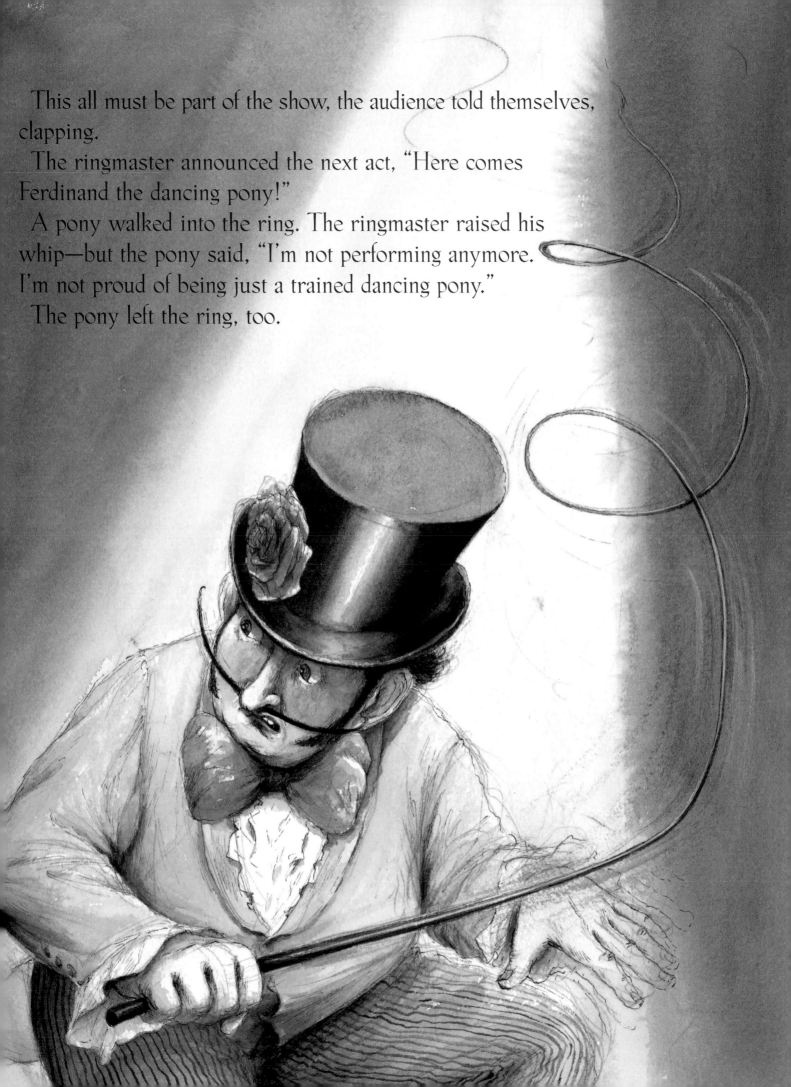

Feeling quite unsure of himself by now, the ringmaster announced the third, fourth, and fifth acts: Louise the giraffe, Augustus the lion, and Otto the dog. They all came into the ring, but none of them would perform.

The giraffe didn't want to do tricks with her long neck. The lion wanted to go back to Africa. And although Otto the dog liked his ball, he didn't like the collar around his neck one little bit.

The ringmaster clutched his head and cried in despair,
"They've all gone on strike! This is rebellion!"

Now the audience began to whistle and jeer, and, complaining, they walked out of the circus.

Meanwhile, the six circus rebels were packing up their belongings and leaving.

By the time the last of the audience came out of the big top, grumbling, the six had disappeared.

They stopped in a wood to rest.

"We're free at last," said Petronius.

"We'll have a lovely life now," said Theodore the donkey, dreamily.

"It'll be tough, too," said Ferdinand the pony, not so dreamily.

"Great artists always have a hard time," said Louise the giraffe.

"But it's easier without a chain around your neck," said Otto the dog.

Petronius stood up, took the dog's chain off, and said, "I know exactly what you mean, Otto."

"Maybe we'll get to Africa sometime," said Augustus the lion.

"We'll look for work tomorrow," said Petronius. "We have to earn enough money to buy ourselves a circus tent and a trumpet."

Everyone agreed. When there was nothing left of the fire but glowing embers, they lay down to sleep, dreaming happily of their very own circus.

The next morning they went off to the nearest little
town, but only Louise and Ferdinand found any work
there. Louise was hired to light the streetlamps every
evening and put them out again at dawn.

"My long neck is just right for this kind of work," she
said, pleased.

Ferdinand was pleased, too. He had taken a job pulling the milk cart to the dairy every morning and every evening. But one day, when the local band happened to pass by playing a waltz on their trumpets, Ferdinand began to dance. The cart tipped sideways, and the milk spilled all over the town square.

Ferdinand lost his job, and he was angry with himself for being a performing pony who couldn't forget the tricks he'd learned.

Ferdinand and Louise hadn't earned enough money for both a circus tent and a trumpet.

"Never mind," said Petronius. "We really don't need a tent. It will be so much nicer to hold our circus out in the fresh air."

The others readily agreed.

Petronius painted some posters, and three days later the
Circus for Children and Poets gave its first performance.
There were children everywhere, and some grown-ups
came, too. It looked as if there must be a lot of poets living
in this town.

Circus for
Children and Poets

Otto played with his striped ball, just the way he did in the old circus—only without a collar around his neck this time.

Petronius blew his trumpet and told stories. Theodore listened happily.

Then Petronius played a waltz for Ferdinand. And this time Ferdinand forgot his tricks and didn't dance. He went to sleep instead. He had always longed to be allowed to sleep right through a waltz.

The children loved the show. They clapped and laughed happily, and so did the grown-ups. They had never seen a circus like this before. Everyone thought it was wonderful!

When the show was over, many of the children came up to congratulate the performers.

One boy went over to Petronius. "You're a very good clown," he said. "Here's my balloon. It's a present for you."

The children and grown-ups went away feeling cheerful. And Petronius and Louise, Otto and Theodore, and Ferdinand and Augustus were very, very happy indeed.